Lost & Found Fiction
4481 Frost St
Nashville, TN, 37214

OLIVE

by
Buchanan Moncure

This book is a work of fiction. Names, characters, places, and incidents are either products of the author's imagination or are used fictitiously. Any resemblance to actual events or locales or persons, living or dead, is entirely coincidental.

Copyright © 2016 by Lost & Found Fiction

All rights reserved, including the right to reproduce this book or portions thereof in any form whatsoever. For information address Lost & Found Fiction at:

us@lostandfoundfiction.com

First edition January, 2016

For wholesale inquiries email us@lostandfoundfiction.com.

Text set in Arial.

Manufactured in the United States of America.

Edited by Mary DeMay.

Front cover imagery from Rider-Waite Tarot Deck, back cover photography by Cameron Beyrent.

This printing is a first edition copy.

LOST & FOUND

Olive

a novella by Buchanan Moncure

To Darling Donna

Buchanan

to Erica, forever my favorite artist

Somewhere there's a universe of missing stuff.

-Lindsay Lohan

PART I:
Remembering the Past

Your voicemail box was always full because of some alcoholic ex-girlfriend who liked to call and leave three hour monologues in your inbox. It cut her off every few minutes, and she never arrived at her point before the inbox was full. So she would write to you, alerting you that you need to clear up some space for new voicemails.

She never bothered you much, but I can't say that I was a fan.

I was always worried that once I was in her position I'd never be able to get a word in, because she would still be going on, talking into her silent receiver about events from the late 90's.

You would give up small amounts of information about her occasionally, but always without revealing too many details. You'd joke that you couldn't talk about it, because perhaps she was famous. Because perhaps she was Courtney Love.

It bothered me so much that I tracked all of Courtney Love's activity on Twitter to see if I could arrange a chance encounter with her. I thought if I could just get a glimpse of her in person, I could quickly mention your name. If this struggling starlet was really so hung up on you, there would be no way that she wouldn't show a response to your name.

Courtney Love tweets a lot, and soon enough I was close to being fired from my minimum-wage job if I didn't stay off of my phone.

I very rarely got any text messages or phone calls on it, it was a device used almost solely for tracking Courtney Love.

You keep a flask under the passenger seat of your Corolla, or at least you did then (I don't know what it is that you do now) and I always took sips from it at stop lights and in standstill traffic. You'd call me an alcoholic, but I'd remind you that I was not the one with a flask in my car.

If I drove, I probably would have driven around with something larger than a flask, anyhow.

There was a thick cloud of cigarette smoke between us as I sat across from you at dinner. I never smoked until I started watching her interviews online, she just made it look so irresistible. I recently had started flirting with my boss; I was in no way interested in my boss, but I also was not in a position to lose my job. I was struggling to settle on a moral position on this, but you weren't concerned by it:

"We'll be out of here soon enough."

I thought I was your captor. It turned out you were the one who'd kidnapped me, and I was stricken with a nearly fatal case of Stockholm Syndrome. I was getting ready to fly to Scandinavia with you, I wanted to forget about every person, place, and object I'd ever known and start a new life with you, surrounded by people who would never accept me as their own and who spoke words in a language I hoped to never understand.

I wanted a life containing nothing but you, and then you disappeared without me.

Some time later, nighttime was no longer for sleeping.

6:00 AM would arrive before I'd even thought about going to bed. I'd been too busy — cutting my bangs, watching ancient sitcoms and scrubbing floor boards.

I'd been busy sorting old love notes by word count.

I'd been busy turning flowers to face the sun, desperately attempting to remember from where it entered the room.

I'd been busy thinking about the night where I was packing my boxes.

Staring at my passport.

Waiting for the moment when I could pretend that America had been a bad dream that I'd woken up from, and almost instantly forgotten. I wasn't telling anyone where I was going, and I wasn't saying goodbye. I was even prepared to unfollow Courtney Love on Twitter.

My phone had died. At that moment I was thinking I

probably wouldn't even bother charging it again. After all, it was one unfollow away from being a completely useless device.

Hidden corridors, spiral staircases, abandoned baggage. These were things that you were always searching for. Holidays were spent traveling, with a keen eye being kept out for your favorite distractions. Conversation made this search too difficult, and radio was out of the question. But on long drives through countrysides and sightless states, conversation flowed as easily as the Norwegian words that would pour out of the mouths of the Scandinavian strangers that would soon surround us.

I thought I wanted a life in a cold place with you, but I ended up with nothing more than a closet full of full-length coats.

"Tell me about the time you fled the cops on roller-skates," you said with your eyes holding a steady gaze on the road ahead.

It was nothing impressive. There is way less traffic on the sidewalks. Especially if you aren't afraid to knock over a few senior citizens.

I didn't really feel this way, but I knew that's what you wanted to hear.

I didn't like to think about the time in my life where running from the police was necessary.

I also couldn't picture the type of life where police lights weren't a terrifying sight.

Tell me about the time you held a chicken, I said, hoping to change the subject.

"It's really not that good of a story."

After too much time spent alone in the apartment that had once been shared, I started to realize how much contempt I held for the city that I'd been calling home. Sure, I had some friends here, but not the type of friends who called or thought of me with any frequency.

These people were somehow rising to fame and I was staying put.

I couldn't decide if this was a good or a bad thing.

I sat in the passenger seat of my friend Alice's car one night as she heard her song on the radio for the first time. She'd told me minutes before that she hadn't heard that final version of the song. It had been emailed to her but she'd turned it off before the introduction had ended. As it started, she pulled to the shoulder of the interstate immediately. I instantly knew what was happening.

The song sounded very different from the demo I'd heard some months earlier, almost unrecognizable, but when the chorus arrived it was very much the same song, only so much more beautiful than before.

I could see why she would be hesitant to hear this. Worried that the song that she knew so intimately would be changed, completed, and brought to ruin, just to then put on display unlike anything she'd ever created before. It was some scary shit.

Olive

The song started to end but disco melodies and slamming piano keys danced along. Alice's eyes were still on the road, her expression and posture unchanged since she'd pulled aside. I stared at her, waiting to see how she would respond. "Well..." she said, finally after what seemed like several minutes had passed.

Well? It's beautiful. It's absolutely beautiful. I can't believe this. I can't believe this is on the radio...it's like... too good for the radio. But not in a pretentious way, it's just so beautiful... Alice, I don't know what to say.

She smirked. "It sounds like you have a lot to say, so don't stop now."

She pulled back onto the road and didn't stop smiling for the rest of the night.

I didn't have many feelings about fame, but I didn't think that it was something I wanted.

I did know I felt an insurmountable desire to create art, and nothing made me feel more alive than witnessing the birth of it.

From the look of things, fame seemed to be the only way to make a living through art. But I was realizing more and more that it wasn't the art itself that made the money.

It was the appearances. The openings, the signings, the tours and gigs and merchandise. To be famous was to be selling postcards of your paintings or MP3s of your songs for a dollar apiece or less if millions of people didn't already know who you were.

I'd quit my minimum-wage job by then, and was instead running a stand at the local farmer's market. Passing off stolen produce as organic and locally grown.

The bored and stoned self-checkout attendee at my local supermarket paid no attention to what item numbers I entered as I rang up my groceries. I rang every thing up as Roma tomatoes for months until I found the codes in the day old section that rang up for just pennies per pound.

This profession, or stand in for the lack of such, allowed me enough time and money to create art. Unfortunately my time spent as a full-time artist and produce-con was spent mostly trying to decide what type of art I should make.

Film? Surely film. Maybe not.

Novels? Too long. Short stories? Too trite.

Painting? Too much talent and too many materials required. Too many messes to clean up.

I ran into a friend at the grocery store while buying avocados, ringing each one up as a day-old baguette. She lit up and shouted:

"Crissy's mom died, but she found a gallery that wants to show her stuff in New York! So she's selling her mom's house and moving to the city, all of her dreams are coming true. I mean aside from her mom dying, but I don't think they were close."

Olive

Crissy had introduced us, and I'd been to her mother's house. My friend's art hung on every wall of that house, but there was nothing she had painted since high school in sight.

"She looks like such a fan, but I hung these up as soon as I finished them in high school and she's just never gotten around to taking them down."

Crissy's high school paintings didn't look much different from her later work. The color pallet had shifted over time, but her style remained distinct and unreplicable. Her mother was old and immobile, with many cats. So many cats. *My god*, I thought, *what did Crissy do with all of those cats.*

Is she taking the cats to New York?

"Does she have a cat? I haven't heard anything about that. Maybe. I wouldn't know."

I passed four crates of organic arugula off as expired parsley and went straight to work.

Life continued on. I continued on. Without you, not as strong or as full of life as once before — but not incapable of survival. Not yet. Perhaps because this was a time when I still held so vividly in my mind the memory of our last shared moment. Before it faded with time. I spent my days running through it, focusing each time on new details in addition to the ones I knew all so well, finding less and less to decipher each time.

"I'm headed out of town for a few days. I'll be back before

you know it."

I had this sneaking suspicion that these would be the last words I'd ever hear you speak.

Two days later when I saw your car on the lot of a dealership full of nearly junk vehicles I knew my suspicions were correct. There was no need to take a closer look at the car to check for distinguishing details — my gut told me all I needed to know. You were gone, and there was nothing I could do about it. You wouldn't be coming back, and I'd be right where you left me, hoping I was wrong.

To avoid setting anyone up for disappointment I will state something clearly now, an action that is new to me: I never saw you again, and I only heard your voice one more time. The story of the last time we spoke is one that I've never told before, but it feels important to include.

I received a blank postcard in the mail a few weeks later with an image of a Tarot card on the front: The Two of Cups.

My address was written upside down.

I put this card in the back of a drawer that I avoided opening. I put it next to my passport, which was only six days away from expiring. I didn't have the money to renew it, and therefore was certain that I wouldn't be able to make use of it anytime soon. Besides, I'd be too busy living a life I'd always hoped to avoid.

Two days later, the reversed two of cups was still haunting me and I stepped out onto the street, directly in front of

Olive

a moving car.

I'd been thinking about suicide nonstop in the days leading up to this, something that felt natural to think about following such drastically disappointing circumstances.

I'd been thinking about it, on an abstract level, but not considering it.

I also didn't consider the car when I stepped into the street, and I can only assume my subconscious was taking my thoughts and running with them.

I woke up in the hospital, with no recollection of how I got there or where my things where.

A doctor came in, explained that I'd been lucky and could go home immediately if I felt comfortable with doing so.

I acknowledged that I understood, and the doctor walked out of the room, closing the door behind himself.

I picked up the phone that rested next to the bed and dialed your number. It was a number that I'd long remembered, in fact the only one that I knew, and dialing it was no more within my control than stepping in front of that car had been.

The phone rang. It stopped. I heard your voice answer.

This was my first time hearing your voice in so long, I took a moment to savor it.

You repeated your salutation into the phone, sounding slightly more annoyed this time.

I'm sorry, I didn't noticed you had answered...

"Is this—"

Yeah, it's me. I figured you'd heard. I just wanted to call to say that everything is okay.

"Heard about what? What happened? I haven't heard anything about you since the last time we spoke...in fact I'm not sure where I would have heard anything about you anyhow."

Oh.

There was a pause. A slightly longer pause than I was comfortable with.

Well, I'm okay. I'm in the hospital. I walked in front of a car but I'll be fine. I'm kind of bruised up. I have the option to stay but I'm probably going to take the bus home. There's nothing to worry about.

"Wait, what? There was an accident?"

There are no accidents, I responded, and hung up the phone.

That was the last sentence I ever spoke to you, and this is the last one I will write to you. From this point forward, my words are intended for someone who will read them.

Still in the hospital, I stood up from the bed and located my things, neatly folded in a nearby chair. I changed back into my clothes, now dirty from the street, and left.

Olive

My phone was still in my pocket, and it started ringing as soon as I walked out of the main door of the hospital. I took it out to notice that the screen had cracked, and behind the crack was the name of a coworker from my old minimum-wage job.

I considered not answering, but then remembered that I was leaving a hospital with no knowledge of what part of town I'd been brought to, nor any medical insurance or money to catch a bus home. It occurred to me that perhaps my old job owed me money, so I answered the call.

"Hey, how are you?"

I've been worse...

"I have some bad news....it's about Blake."

My heart sunk.

Blake had been another coworker of our's at that job, he was one of the few people there worth knowing and I hadn't seen him since I left to start selling stolen fruits and vegetables. Blake was younger than I was. Really young.

"I'm sorry to tell you this over the phone...I'd just hate for you to read it online or in the newspaper...Blake killed himself last night."

My heart stopped.

I had no words to speak into the phone, so I thanked my coworker for calling and hung up. I went back into the hospital and informed the receptionist that I'd decided to stay the night after all.

By the end of the next day, I made it home.

Blake's death left me feeling heavier than ever before. I entered my apartment with an awareness of this fact, and I knew that this heaviness meant that Blake's death had more of an impact on me than he could have imagined.

I know that, in the grand scheme of things, I wasn't that important in his life. And, had he not died, he probably wouldn't have been very important in my own. But this status of importance was not worth the loss of him, and this made me realize that I would never have the option of suicide...no matter how bad things got.

This knowledge that there was no escaping life terrified me, and was far scarier than the thought of suicide ever had been.

I found a jar of olives in the back of the cabinet that night, and I held one in my mouth until I fell asleep.

I woke up choking.

PART II:
Living in the Present

I'm eating olives now, and that's about it.

Green or black, jarred or canned, soaked in vodka or gin.

I'm averaging 24 olives per day, with the occasional slice of fruit or blade of grass to supplement the nutrients that I'm surely neglecting.

This is no metaphor, this really happened.

This is really happening.

It is happening to me.

My skin is delicate and precious, like a Faberge egg. Exposure to the sun could ruin me, causing cracks and blemishes, so here I remain. Sitting in the barren-most corner of my kitchen, consuming alcohol soaked olives by the cupful.

Going to sleep has been replaced by passing out, falling cold with clammy skin and a blurry mind. I can't stand the taste of food or water or other beverages these days.

Olive

I'm making the best of my current situation.

I'm longing for loneliness. Solitude. A life spent alone. I fear that as soon as I have it I'll lose my mind, but is a mind that's lost worse than one that's troubled and cluttered?

I'm thinking about making art, and I'm worrying that I think about it more than I do it.

Dreaming has been replaced with tosses and turns, actions that I'm too far from consciousness to recognize, but feel upon waking. My pillows have become a burden, and I'm thinking about throwing them all into the river:

Two shirts.

Two pillows.

Any item that reminds me of a lover that has long disappeared, a lover that probably spends his days inside of Courtney Love's smoke-filled apartment. Salt and pepper shakers that are impossible to refill and make me feel like a failure, I'll throw all of these items into the river and watch them wash away.

In the shower, nothing seems to wash away anymore. Dirt may disappear momentarily, but the bags under my eyes and the weight on my shoulders remain unchallenged.

Summer is heavy in the air.

The art that I long to create remains at bay.

I want to see the whole world without having to go as

far as the edge of my own backyard. I want to taste the booze soaked olives of each country, pungent flavors that will help hide the dryness of antidepressants and painkillers and paint chips that I held in my mouth as a child.

I want to experience life at its fullest, feeling every high and embracing every low.

I want to do this all from the comfort of my home, while avoiding the temptation to live vicariously through the posts and photos that crowd my computer screen from every stupid fucking person I went to high school with.

I want to believe that the past never happened, that the future isn't daunting and death will never arrive.

But I know more than I care to, and I know that 6,098 people die every hour and the odds are stacked against me.

Besides, I've never had any luck with gambling.

My life is hungover, full of aches and pains and fogginess that I just can't shake. There is something stuck in my stomach, like the pits of the olives that I swallow all day long.

The river behind my house is filling up with my possessions, and I'm sure that soon enough I won't have anything left to give.

Nothing but empty jars, cans and liquor bottles.

Olive

The apartment that I'll be calling home now belongs to my friend Shirley. She's an alcoholic who spends most of her time with her boyfriend, who I will never meet. Sometimes I won't see her for weeks at a time.

Once my bags were packed and my lease was ending and Norway was nothing but a forgotten dream, I had to come up with a new exit strategy, and fast. Shirley and I had been in and out of touch for years, and when I called and suggested that I get on buses until I arrived at her house she was extremely supportive of the idea.

"I barely even live at my house, you can have it. I don't even need rent, just water the plants."

So I left. It looked like this:

Tea in Chicago at 6:01 AM after a ten hour bus ride.

All of my belongings were on an Amtrak train on the other side of the country, slowly catching up with me on my journey to Milwaukee.

Following two blue sleeping pills and two giant pot brownies, I still managed to get only 13 minutes of cumulative sleep.

A construction worker complemented me on my unwashed hair, and I was unsure if he was being sincere or sarcastic.

Buchanan Moncure

I said thank you.

I walked with certainty, convinced I could play the role of a native since all of the locals on the bus had assumed as much.

I'd never been there before, and I spent just 119 minutes before my next bus was scheduled to arrive.

Earl Grey with honey and lemon will never fail me.

My internal compass will never lead me in the right direction.

Union Station was a 10 minute walk from where I started, and I allowed myself 45 minutes of trial and error on my way back.

I'd just barely missed my bus as I arrived at the station, but thankfully a train departed in 30 minutes from the same block, and it only cost me a third of the money in my bank account.

On the bus to Chicago I'd sat at the window seat.

From departure until Louisville a man sat next to me who never spoke.

I had to excuse myself past him to use the rest room four times during these three hours.

From there to Indianapolis, I had the seat to myself while a loud-mouthed man and a short-tempered young girl argued relentlessly behind me.

Olive

In Indianapolis, a friendly but giant older woman with a thick African accent placed herself next to me. She continuously threw heavy luggage into my lap, always asking if I would mind holding them immediately after.

I complied.

Now on the train to Milwaukee, I watched the sun illuminate Chicago and found myself in awe of the city while simultaneously hoping to never see it again.

I ate an olive and said goodbye to the windy city.

Finally, on a nearly empty train car, I managed more than a few minutes of sleep.

When I arrived in Milwaukee (much later than intended) Shirley was sitting on the hood of her car, chain smoking cigarettes. We hugged.

"I've locked myself out of my apartment until my friend with the extra key gets off of work, but I can show you around in the meantime."

Shirley continued chain smoking as she sped down the interstate, paying no mind to the road in front of her.

"That's where my friend Janey Stills killed herself," she said, pointing to the fifth column of the bridge that we were speeding down. "Hung herself. How inconsiderate can you be? If you want to kill yourself on a bridge be my guest, but just go ahead and fucking jump. Hanging yourself? Do that shit at home. I never did like her."

She's right. Poor Janey. Always dying for the spotlight,

and her end came suspended over Lake Michigan. Oh the final sights she could have seen had only she hung herself from the opposite side.

I didn't actually feel bad for Janey, my thoughts were with the poor city employee who had to remove her swollen body from the bridge the next morning as cars and bitterly-cold air rushed past.

"Me?" Shirley says, "I'm content here in Milwaukee. You won't catch me throwing myself over any bridges. A few years ago...maybe. But not since I made it here. Everything works out. If it worked out for me it will sure as shit work out for you too."

The word content curdled something inside of me.

A fear of contentness aside, I needed to hear these words. And I knew that Shirley believed them, but I couldn't help but think that she knew it's what I need to hear too. That being said, I didn't believe it.

"Coming up on the left is city hall — can you see that clock tower?"

I saw it, in all of its classic glory. And the time was only off by ten minutes.

"Dozens of people kill themselves in there each year. They just take all of their problems to city hall and call it a day. Unload. Not a bad way to go if you ask me."

Our suicide tour concluded at Potawatomi Casino, at 2:00 PM on a Tuesday. Rows and rows of elderly woman with their cigarettes, oxygen tanks and bingo cards lined the halls, all slowly drifting into sight as we traveled up the escalator.

I spent the last of my cash on nickel slots and quickly learned that my luck was not going to be found in a casino. Not today, at least.

"Okay. Suicide tour over, this is bringing me down. Let's go to the lake."

Today is Tuesday.

I remind myself of this on the ride to the lake.

Today is Tuesday.

Tomorrow will be Wednesday.

I had a feeling that Thursday would be the end of the world, but I also felt like I'd live to see the weekend.

"We fly kites here when it's warm out — there is a kite store right over there but I've never been inside."

I've never flown a kite.

I've never been camping.

I've never kissed a stranger.

These are all things I would regret should the world have ended that Thursday, but I wasn't in a position to change them.

I've never touched a frog.

I've never seen a crocodile.

Or a giraffe.

Or a zebra.

These were things that I was in no hurry to change.

Shirley's phone rang, she answered without saying hello.

"How many times do I have to tell you? Don't call me before 11:00 AM, and I don't answer my phone between 3:00 and 5:00 PM. And for god's sake don't call me after 6:30 PM, that's fucking inappropriate."

She hung up.

You realize you're leaving a very small window of time for phone calls?

"Are you complaining?"

Certainly not. Who was that?

"I don't have a clue."

I quickly tried to mentally memorize the schedule that she had just screamed into the phone. Exhausted by this, I decided maybe I should just let Shirley call me.

Shirley threw her cigarette on the ground and we walked back to the car.

Olive

When Shirley's friend Steve finally got off work, he met us at the house and let us in. "Here, you should have this now," he said, handing me the key. "I'm sick of letting her in all of the time."

"I haven't seen my keys in months," Shirley said, shuffling through an unimaginably tall stack of envelopes and magazines that had crowded the mailbox.

Shirley's apartment was quaint, but nice. "This is your home now, feel free to do as you please," she said, throwing the entire stack of envelopes into the overflowing garbage can, and laying the magazines on the coffee table. "The bathroom is at the end of the hall, my bedroom is to the left, yours is to the right. If that room isn't big enough for you we could switch...but it's going to take me a while to clear out my things. Actually, I think it will be big enough for you. When do your things arrive?"

I held up the small carry on bag that had been anchoring me down for the last two days,

It's pretty much all right here.

My clothes no longer fit, they hung on me, making me look like some child in adult's clothing. So I donated them to charity and grabbed a few shirts out of the suitcase that the lover who had surely forgotten me by now had left at my house, for the event of last minute travel. I have a knack for convincing people to take long, spur of the moment trips in the middle of the night.

Fuck your job, let's go to New Orleans, I'd say.

He'd tell me it was the craziest idea I'd ever had, but sure enough we'd arrive by sunrise.

He never quit his job, he just killed off family members one at a time. By the end of the year his coworkers had taken up a collection to offer him as a bonus, some sort of cosmic apology for the hard year that he'd had.

A hard year of being downwind from my cigarette smoke while watching the sun rise over the gulf.

Luck was found in casinos in New Orleans that year, but never again.

I later found out he spent the bonus on a one way ticket out of where we were, on a plane with no room for me.

"Well, take anything you need from my room. Like I said, I'm not here much, so I'll probably never miss it." Shirley said. She hugged me and looked deep into my eyes, surely spotting the sorrow that had overwhelmed me for so long, she smiled, "Maybe you should get a cat."

After Shirley left I unpacked my things: my olives, my T-shirts, my sleeping pills, ancient laptop and uncharged phone.

Finally, I ventured into Shirley's room. At first the door wouldn't open, and I thought for a moment that it may have been locked. I quickly realized this wasn't the case, and that something was just blocking the way. I pushed hard against the door, making use of all of my body weight, as little as that may have been.

Olive

Finally it opened, and the source of the door's resistance became immediately apparent.

In the middle of the room there was a queen size bed, but it took me several minutes to realize this. My view was obstructed by piles and piles of...*stuff*...it covered every inch. What kind of stuff? Who knows, the kind that all blends together in an overwhelming way. Papers, products that had never been removed from their clamshell packaging, paintings, books, more books, and more clothes than you'd find in any department store. This massive amount of *stuff* made all of the floor appear to be on the same level of bed, which was covered completely in magazines.

Like me, Shirley had always preferred the company of the written word to that of other people. I'd spent years convincing myself that words and flowing water are all the company that I needed. I plugged in my phone, after days of being dead it finally turned on, displaying one unread message from Shirley:

"There is a river five blocks east of the house."

I walked to the river, immediately feeling slightly more alive by the sound of the rushing water.

Alive enough to make it through the night.

The Amtrak train with the my remaining belongings would never arrive.

After a week and a few days, on a Friday, Shirley convinced me for the first time to leave the house — to go to a party.

Not wanting to be a bad house mate, I complied.

I didn't know what I expected, but the party was oddly upscale. My unbrushed hair and stained tennis shoes did not fit in.

There were cocktails and hors d'oeuvres, including olives which I immediately piled onto my plate amongst corners of bread and discarded lemon wedges from my gin.

At the party, while on new and unidentifiable drugs, a few different colored pills handed to me on the car ride over, I told strangers that I was writing a novel. This was a lie. I was not writing a novel, I was merely talking about it. And sometimes I would think about it, but I'd yet to start writing said novel. I hadn't even thought about characters or plots or endings or intentions. I ate an olive, I offered one to a stranger and hoped they would decline.

They did not.

I find myself back at home, still high and unsure of how I got there. This was happening more and more, losing moments and days and occasionally weeks. I lost May of last summer, but I can say with some degree of certainty that nothing important happened.

I turned on a camera that I found in Shirley's room, I turned it to face myself. I zoomed in on my mouth and lit a cigarette. A tear fell down my face, though my eyes were out of view. I asked myself:

Olive

Is this art?

Surely not.

I ate another olive.

When I walked to the river the next night I passed a sign that had been posted. It was printed on normal paper, and it is clear to me that it was made by a concerned citizen, and not some government official. It read:

STOP DUMPING YOUR BELONGINGS HERE.

YOU CANNOT PLACE YOUR PERSONAL BURDENS ON NATURE.

Tonight, this sign was the only thing that I threw in.

An old, large orange cat showed up on a Wednesday. Who could say what week this was. I opened the door to walk to the river and she let herself in, immediately purring and rubbing herself against my legs. I accepted her as a gift, named her Tomato, and decided to buy her food.

At the store near the house, the clerk eyed me as if I were some sort of shoplifter. I'd never stolen anything from here. I'd stolen plenty in my life, but the days of pocketing physical items were long behind me. Despite this, I decided that I couldn't shop here anymore. I placed my basket full of olives, canned tuna and paper towels on the floor next to the door and walked out.

From now on I'd do my shopping online.

In an attempt to do this, I opened the social websites that I'd worked so hard to avoid.

I learned that today Kara packed up her possessions and preschooler and left her husband and the life that she had built behind.

I learned that Chris lost his job. That Casey Kasem died.

None of these things affected me in any way, but they were all too much to process. I packed my computer and power cord, my laptop case and headphones. I walked to the river and threw them all in.

My apartment was becoming emptier and emptier, and I was hoping that, with time, my mind would follow suite. I'd stopped entering Shirley's room, too afraid of betraying her kindness and taking her possessions for a swim. Not that she'd miss them. If I thought that I could carry the couch five blocks on my own I would throw it in, too. But in my current state I knew this to be impossible.

I could barely lift the cat, and while I'd tried to share olives with this friend she was not interested. I could no longer buy canned tuna at the store near my house, and I could not order online without a computer.

I opened the door and waited for the cat to leave. It took a few hours, but eventually she did — just more than a week after she arrived.

I'd always felt a strong psychic connection to the animals in my life, the same connection that I tried so hard to force onto every human that I ever loved. This connection died out around the second time that the cat denied my offering of Kalamata olives, and I realized I could no longer offer her the life that she deserved.

The next night I unplugged the microwave from the wall. I assume this appliance came with the apartment, and was therefore not mine nor Shirley's to throw away. I walked to the river, a task that is much easier without a small appliance in tow. After five blocks and seven breaks I reached my destination, and I slammed the microwave against a rock before throwing it into its new home.

Another night, another party.

I should say, before arriving in the Midwest I'd never *really* been one for drugs. Every now and then a puff of pot had made me feel better, often after 1 or 2 too many drinks. It helped me sleep, slowing my mind to a state where I could not keep up with my racing thoughts. Mostly it made me feel like I was in high school again, and reminded me of how lucky I was to be so far removed from that time.

So, at Shirley's friend Erin's birthday party I drank too much gin. I drank, in fact, a pint of gin. I just poured the entire bottle into my oversized cup and kept drinking.

There were drugs here. Many drugs.

This didn't bother me, I had been around them many times and have never been phased. Once, a few years earlier, I drank a tea made of mushrooms and made snow angels in the gravel behind my townhome. It was great in the moment, but the next day was pretty painful.

There were people doing cocaine to my left — a drug that to me had always seemed sad. Overwhelmingly so.

And maybe alcohol and pot and mushroom tea are sad too, but I've always felt a definite division.

But people do what they will.

I was propped in a corner now, Shirley had stepped outside. Shirley was a friend who was much better in social situations than I. Everyone I knew fell into this category, but especially Shirley.

I'd been using Shirley as a crutch, remaining in the same group as her all night and contributing to her stories in lieu of telling my own or listening to others.

This was an old dance for Shirley and I.

She left for the car to take a phone call and I propped myself in the corner.

I checked my phone and there were messages, but they quivered on the cracked screen.

I couldn't focus on the words. I did not read them, I just stared blankly in an attempt to convince others that I was.

"Who's messaging you?" a stranger to my left asked.

No one important, just Courtney Love, I say jokingly,

knowing it was probably not a joke. I put the phone back into my pocket.

"Do you smoke weed?" Asked the stranger that I now recognize as Erin's roommate.

Oh, yeah. Sure.

What happened next confused me.

He handed me a tall glass bong, filled to the rim with ice.

"Just wait," he whispered, and he began to light it with a tiny blowtorch that seemingly appeared out of nowhere.

"Ok, now pull."

I was drunk and making new friends, so I didn't protest or ask questions.

I deeply inhaled, breathing in the ice cold air until finally he placed a toothpick to the now bright red metal bowl.

Now, I don't know what I was expecting, but what came next took me by surprise.

My lungs filed, overfilled actually, with a smoke that burned like a chemical. It did not taste nor feel natural or healthy at all, and I felt indescribable pain as it expanded in my lungs. It felt as if the chemicals were eating away at my chest. As I exhaled I felt as if I'd never be able to breathe or speak again.

I immediately felt the need to vomit.

I kept coughing, short unproductive coughs that only made things worse. They did nothing but reiterate the pain that had consumed my chest and throat, and prevented air from finding its way in.

Erin's roommate laughed madly, and between coughs I said *There is no way this is pot*, but he was laughing too hard to bring any words to the surface.

His laughter was more uncontrolled than my coughing.

My world had been turned upside down, and I mean this literally.

My feet felt higher than my head, like being stuck upside down on some broken down roller coaster, or being tied up and dangling from the ceiling. Perhaps I was.

The room was still full of the thick chemical smoke. Everything smelled like gasoline and I felt extremely ill.

Somehow, I stumbled outside.

It was my intention to smoke a cigarette. Despite the pain in that remained in my chest I felt that this activity would help me remember how to breathe.

Unfortunately this never actually happened.

The world was still upside down, I was still feeling like I'd been exposed to chemical warfare, and the cold air hit my skin — immediately bringing sweat to the surface.

Suddenly people started asking me questions and awaiting responses. But it took all that I had just to sink into a lawn chair. Eventually they'd learn to seek answers elsewhere.

The world kept spinning, while I remained still at the bottom of it — trying to find the best way to come up for air.

No one was practicing any self-control here, and as far gone as I found myself I guess I'm not one to speak. I suppose I was doing about as good as anyone else, but this didn't seem to comfort me.

Instead I was scared. There needed to be more control. I needed to be at home, eating olives and thinking about the past.

I needed someone present who was competent enough to prevent any potentially traumatic decisions.

Knowing this element of control was not present scared me. It scared me so much that, suddenly, I felt that I was in grave danger.

I had to leave, and as soon as I could get out of the lawn chair I intend to do so.

Drugs make time so hard to track. So it's hard for me to say exactly how long I was stranded in the lawn chair. I do know that it felt like days, and it was surely hours.

Or perhaps not — by the time I regained the ability to stand I started to rush. I started bumping into people and forgetting my things and doing whatever it took to find my way out of the front door and back to Shirley's car.

After much stumbling and a fair amount of falling I found my way to the car, where Shirley was finishing her bourbon in the passenger's seat.

She unlocked the doors.

I need to start off by saying I'm not doing too well, I said while climbing into the driver's seat of the SUV. These were the first words that I'd spoken since I landed in the lawn chair.

"Oh you're fine, I've seen you drink way more than that."

No, Shirley, no. I don't know what I did. Erin's roommate is an evil fuck, at this point I was still sweating bullets and yanking at my hair.

"Who, Kyle? He's an interesting character — that's for sure," Shirley said, turning her glass pint up to reach the final drops of booze.

No Shirley, he's evil. He tricked me. I think I smoked crack.

Within a second of when these words left my lips Shirley had slung her door open, smashed her bottle on the road, and found her way to my left side.

"Get up. We're going inside and I'm going to kick his ass. Tell me everything."

I assured her that an ass kicking would do no good. Mostly I wanted to avoid returning to the party at all costs.

I told her everything. The blow torch, the chemical burn,

the smell of gasoline.

"I don't know what I was thinking... I should have known better... I thought maybe it was hash at worst. But really I wasn't thinking at all…"

Shirley hugged me and held me tight, I rested my tired and heavy body against the steering wheel with my head on her shoulder.

"I don't think you smoked crack. I have no idea what you smoked but just try to relax. A negative headspace isn't going to make things any better."

I attempted to take in as much of Shirley's good energy as possible. She was, in this town, my longest standing friendship. By default.

Several states had separated us for some time, but suddenly it had been six months since I packed up what was left of my apartment and had nowhere to go once Scandinavia had been so suddenly taken off the table. I took a bus to Shirley's house, and I'd been living there ever since. We had a judgement-free friendship and I was caring for her plants while she nurtured her relationship with Eric, a boy I was now sure I'd never meet.

I sent a series of incomprehensible text messages to my only other friend in the city. His name was Travis, I met him by the river one night and ignored him. On the third night of avoiding his eyes while I tossed small things in he came over and asked what I was doing.

Have you ever posted a sign on that tree, I said, pointing the tree where the sign that had haunted me had been hung.

"No. I just come here to write."

I didn't tell him that I was writing a novel, instead I told him that I'd been throwing things into the river as a form of art.

"I like the sound of that...in what way exactly is it art?"

I'm calling it that.

"Fair enough," he said, and slowly but surely we became friends. Soon enough he'd joined Shirley and Courtney Love in sending messages to my phone, but I'd never seen him away from the river. He told me he lived nearby, and that we should see each other away from the rapids sometime, but I simply changed the subject.

When I'm in an altered state I oftentimes feel the need to let those closest to me know that I'm still alive. At 2:00 AM, most of my friends don't feel the need to know this.

After months like this, where my mind is heavy from drinking daily and smoking whatever is handed to me, I can become a pretty exhausting friend.

Eventually, with the help of ambient music, fresh air, and finally few cigarettes — I started to feel slightly more human.

Despite this, I was still feeling extremely drunk.

Shirley and I set alarms for every ten minutes until

Olive

sunrise, waking up each time to make sure we were both still alive and still too drunk to drive home.

By the time the sun rose we had long overslept our last dozen alarms, and I awoke to a the sight of a large woman outside of the passenger window, watching Shirley's chest rise and fall with each breath.

I felt her gaze before even opening my eyes, and I locked eyes with her as soon as I lifted my eyelids.

Wake the fuck up. Someone is here, I said, slinging my arm and hitting Shirley on the shoulder.

Shirley locked eyes with the stranger as well, who turned and walked away from the car.

At this time I noticed she was holding a leash, attached to a very large dog. A dog that was now peeing on the same tree that I had peed on just hours earlier.

The time was 7:48 AM and my foot had been resting on the gas pedal all night.

We quickly switched seats and drove home.

A few days passed, and at noon — with the sun shining brightly into my room and draining me of any energy that sleep had offered, my phone rang. For the first time in a very long time, I find myself answering my phone.

It was Travis. He wanted me to meet him at the river.

I really can't, I only go there at night…

"I'll see you here in ten minutes." He hung up the phone.

I stumbled into Shirley's room, threw on some clothes with the tags still on and left the house.

Being outside during the day was a new experience for me. I was not used to the penetrating heat of the sun, I worried that I'd burn or maybe melt. I should have worn sunscreen, not that I had any, but surely there was some to be found in Shirley's room.

When I arrived some 35 minutes after his call, Travis was sitting on the rock that I knew all too well. The same one that had been used for smashing microwaves and other breakable objects.

I sat next to him.

"It's nice being outside during the day, isn't it?"

Not especially, I said, reaching into his pocket and fishing out a lighter. I lit a cigarette and blew the smoke high into the sky. I realized he was smoking a joint. He noticed me eyeing it.

"Here, trade me," he said, handing me the joint. I handed him my cigarette and took the joint, showing some resistance before putting it to my lips.

This…this isn't crack is it?

He laughed, "I've never smoked crack, and the fact that you think you smoke it in joints tells me you haven't either."

Olive

I took a deep drag and held the smoke in my lungs for exactly seven seconds before exhaling.

Can you smoke it from a bong, using a blow torch?

"Um...I'm not really sure. That doesn't sound right, but it's hard to say. You should Google that."

I don't have Google anymore.

He laughed, returned my cigarette and held the joint between his index and middle fingers. "We all have Google, some of us just choose not to use it." He pointed to the river, "Do you see that?"

I looked down, and against two rocks I saw a several items. A microwave. A book (*a bible? I couldn't tell*), and something else that I couldn't identify.

Well...I know that microwave...but those other items are a mystery to me. I don't know who did that.

"I do."

You?

He nodded.

I didn't know what to feel. Oddly honored. Slightly enraged. Completely confused.

I don't understand, I said, still staring at the third item trying to identify what it is.

"You've inspired me to create art, but I've never been

much of an artist so I thought I'd give your medium a try."

I decided to feel moved, and I felt a few tears build up in my eyes. *You're an artist. Never forget it. The world would be incomplete without your writing…*

"You've never read my writing," he said, offering me the joint again.

Travis took my glasses off of my face and cleaned them using his shirt. An act I'd attempted many times without ever seeing any success.

He returned them to my face, and his own face came into vision. Spotless.

Seeing clearly now, I asked Travis if he liked olives and brought him back to my house.

Travis is struck by my home, or more so by the now barren state of it.

"These are all of the things you have?" he asked, surveying the room.

This is all I have. Things aren't that important, I moved here with a small suitcase full of things, that's all. I had some more stuff on a train but it never arrived.

The apartment now contained only a couch, a wobbly coffee table, Shirley's many potted plants and, of course, her very full bedroom.

Come, look at this, I said, grabbing him by the hand and pulling him down the hallway. The touch of his hand is my second human contact in the state of Wisconsin, the first being Shirley's hug. I felt an unfamiliar magnetism in his skin. *This is my roommate Shirley's room,* I pushed hard until the door finally opened.

"Wow. What could she possibly need all of this for?"

I don't know, nuclear apocalypse? She doesn't need any of this stuff, I've never seen her here for more than 10 minutes at a time — and I've never seen her come into this room.

Travis navigated his way through the room and began to shuffle through the piles of magazines that filled Shirley's bed. "These go back years," he said, carefully inspecting the dates.

Magazines and bills are the only thing that ever arrived in the mail here. Each time they came, I forced myself into Shirley's room and filed them away into their home among friends.

Redbook.

Ladies' Home Journal.

Reader's Digest.

Men's Health.

I told Travis to take a few home, to report back when he can tell me what he'd learned.

I hug him at the door. I hold the hug for a long time, an amount of time that I can tell is probably considered too long. I want to kiss him, but the direction in which he pulls away makes it clear that this will not happen.

By the time he leaves the sun is down, and for the first time in a long time I fall right to sleep.

In my dreams, I'm throwing magazines into the river. Dozens and dozens of magazines.

Months and months of Reader's Digest, Time, TV Guide, Soap Opera Weekly, Oprah.

As I do this I hear sirens behind me, and the river that I've come to know so well is illuminated by blue lights.

I want an olive.

I do not have the energy to run from the police, and it is becoming more and more clear that I am who they seek. My roller skates have long been washed downshore.

I step back onto the rock that I've smashed so many possessions into over the last several months and, with grace, I allow myself to fall forward.

The next morning, I wake up and fall right back to sleep. I dream again. This time I'm right here where I was left.

The person who left me? They'd been to Belgium, Brussels and Bangladesh since I saw them, but I'd been rooted here firmly in the same old apartment. Waiting, just like I said I would. *I'll be here,* and here I remain.

And sure, I've seen some sights since I saw them last. The back of police cars, the inside of hospitals, but no matter where I went my mind was right here.

Waiting for the day when I could once again be reeled in.

I don't like to think of myself as a dependent person, but I am undoubtedly a person of my word.

To help me survive the summers when I was growing up, my mother convinced that was allergic to the sun, that stepping outside would be the end of me. Really she was just too afraid of the world and its inhabitants. Terrified that if she let me out into the world I'd see what a mess she was and never come back — just like everyone else.

Another night, another trip to the river.

I threw the toaster in this night, and resisted the growing urge to follow it.

My head was clogged and cloudy.

My thoughts were incoherent and primarily violent. My desires were unreturned, placed back into my mailbox, unopened, with sloppy lettering that read:

return to sender.

Why do we only want that which we cannot have?

Why do we ruin good things in an attempt to grasp the unreachable?

Why do we expect so much from others but give so little in return?

And why does so little feel like so fucking much?

How is it that a few seconds of bad decisions can complicate several years of hard work? And why do others try and comfort us by saying everything is okay when everything is so obviously shattered?

My life was in more pieces than my mother's China doll collection after I knocked it off the shelf as a child. It was a simple mistake, or at least the first doll was. But then I knocked down each one, the entire collection, doll by doll by doll. Smashing each one and cutting my feet on the shards as I attempted to ruin them further.

Ruining the possessions of others should never feel so satisfying, and it never does in the moments that follow.

Regret comes crashing in like a small appliance in a river. Fear washes me away faster than the currents.

Remember to breathe.

Remember to eat.

Remember to say please when asking questions of the universe.

Remember to spit out the pits of olives.

Remember to look both ways when crossing the street.

Remember not to kill myself.

Remember how: Take an olive out of the jar, using your thumb and forefinger. Place it in your mouth and slide it under your tongue like a pill that will take away life's troubles. Spend the rest of your life waiting for the effects.

PART III:
Predicting the Future

There is a spirit that possesses me. When it's late and my neighbors are sleeping and I've been pretending to do so for hours.

It comes knocking at my window and drags me out onto the roof. Forcing me to take a long look at the surroundings that I've happened into.

It's violent and inarticulate, just like the thoughts that race through my head during every second of my waking life. And twice as fast during my sleeping life, when I'm too caught up in anxiety to achieve the rest that I long for during every minute of my day.

The thoughts that say: *Kiss the boy. Touch his face. Throw caution to the wind. Before it's too late. What's the worst that could happen? You ruin everything? You've already ruined everything more times than you can count, so if you fuck this one up why believe you won't live to see another day?*

The spirit is telling me: *Jump,* but just like my thoughts I'm able to control this violent ghost. I'm able to push it to the back of my head, and continue to make safe choices that will allow me to see the age of 30. But... what if I don't?

What if I step off the edge?

It's not that far, only the second story. I may break a bone or two, but why not break the few parts of myself that haven't been broken before?

So, one day, maybe, I'll kiss the boy. I'll touch his thigh and I'll invite him into a world where I'm more than just the least sane person he knows. And if he declines my invitation, he'll just be the most recent in a long line of people who will never speak to me again. No different from any person on the other side of a counter, any friend that I erased from my life like our years of history never occurred. I still see them all, on late nights spent on the goddamn Internet, all 8 letters of their names glowing on the left side of my email. No one worth knowing ever had a name shorter than 9 letters anyhow. 12 if we're being completely honest. Take for example: C-O-U-R-T-N-E-Y L-O-V-E.

And no spirit was ever satisfied with their chosen host climbing back into the window — breaking ledges and coffee cups and tearing down curtains on their way in. And this is what happens as I attempt to escape the ghost, by the way, all of these things break. Leaving a thick layer of drywall dust and ceramic shards in my bed.

The message is clear:

There will be no going to sleep tonight.

Besides, escaping possession has never been as easy as turning around.

Despite how often I try and tell myself the opposite, I'm certain that nothing will ever be enough. No job will ever be a delicate enough balance to keep me fed and not make me feel like I've sold my soul. I'll always think my art is shit, and will never believe someone is doing more than trying to be nice when they say otherwise. I'll always be unhappy with my surroundings, and I'll never have a friend that I won't grow to hate... if I don't already hate them the day we meet.

I'll never devote enough time to my responsibilities, and as soon as I feel responsible for my passions they will eat away at my soul, taking large ineloquent bites.

The spirit whispers in my ear that *no drug, no boy, no rebirth or sunset that will ever feel as good as finally letting go of inhibition*. And though I've spent my entire life pretending to do just that, I'm still waiting on the day where I follow through. Even though there's no going back, what is it that I'm so afraid of not being able to go back to? A mess of -nesses?

Discontent-ness? Loneli-ness? Lazi-ness and maybe some apathy and soap operas? A world where no one has ever said *I love you* expect for in the past tense. Shitty alcohol and awkward parties and trying to dance like no one is watching when you know good and damn well that everyone has their eyes on nothing but you.

They'll always be trying to figure you out. They don't care who you are, but more so why you're here, and why you bothered to leave your house. And don't worry strangers, I feel the same way. Destined to stay inside like some forgotten pet, waiting for its owner to return home.

And with all this luck you've had, the spirit says, *why can't you ever create anything that is as happy as you should be*. And yes, there have been many hard times. But goddamn if there hasn't been a lot of luck that I've forgotten.

There has always been magic in the air, though usually slightly out of focus.

And the answer to the spirit's question is simple, but hard to put into words. There are already so many expressions of happiness in this world, and how could I possibly help spread this lie that one day things all work out nicely?

The spirit invites me back onto the roof. *Time for one more look over the edge. One more cigarette, maybe one more shooting star if I'm lucky*. But I'm still in bed, questioning everything. Questioning whether or not I've misinterpreted every moment of my life up until this point. Maybe the ghost is cold and just wants to be invited inside.

I'm self-destructing. Rapidly working to destroy everything that I've spent so long to build. The only way to be productive is to tear down the home that you've forged. When you change everything to finally find happiness, only to see the same problems that have been staring you in the face for your entire life, what else is there to do?

I'm unraveling, this is one of the only things I'm certain of anymore.

The people who have been around for the longest are one of the targets of my rage. Since I live a life spent mostly alone, I'm at the top of this list of people who are subjected to rage. I can't stand to see myself in the mirror, and anyone facing me by choice surely cannot be trusted.

Friends can only disappoint you. You can put people on pedestals, but you're the only person that gets hurt when it all comes crumbling down.

In the rubble, all you'll ever find is your own reflection.

My hair is falling out strand by strand. My teeth are slowly chipping away. My skin, which has never been plagued, has suddenly turned on me. Maybe because I haven't eaten in four days. If needed, my libido would be nonexistent. And if I can't get it up for myself then how could I possibly do the same for anyone else? My weight is too low, yet I can't shake the desire to shed half of my body.

I'm crawling out of my skin, much too quickly to grow a new one in enough time.

It didn't even take a year for this place to become a thing to be hated like all surroundings that preceded it. I worry that no matter where I go this will be an issue.

I drunk dial an old friend, one who is usually far too busy to take my calls. And I don't blame her.

Olive

She says: "You have this inexplicable ability to make a family no matter where you go, and to stay in one place for too long would be a disservice to that gift."

But what is family if not people that you grow to hate and resent?

I ignore my mother's phone calls. I long for the day when she'll stop trying to reach me to remind me of money owed and promises broken.

I check my bank account. No matter how many days I go without eating I will still never have enough money to buy a car or bus ticket and leave without looking back.

No matter how many months I take off, I'll never feel rested enough to work another day in my life.

Eventually I run out of money. A large check had appeared in my bank account a few weeks after my arrival — completely by surprise, perhaps a bank error in my favor. In fact, it was a deposit from the minimum-wage job from so long ago, and the importance of my intuition that they owed me money was not lost on me. This money lasted a long time, because what do you spend money on if not rent, bills and food?

Now penniless, I begin work as a phone psychic. An idea that comes to me, as if in its own psychic vision. At first it seems as ideal as any job could be: Sit at home. Answer the phone when it rings. Lie to people.

It quickly becomes apparent that it is so much exactly like any corporate job in the world.

I am paid a tiny amount of money compared to the money that my callers pay. I can only get 18 hours of work per week, 8 of which are all full of meetings with disappointed CEOs who urge us to keep callers on the line no matter what the cost.

'If you're losing them, go with either a new romantic opportunity or the death of someone close to them. Listen closely to their words and tone to determine which of these will be more useful for caller retention.'

These meetings are over the phone, with the entire company on one giant conference call.

My phone is muted during the meetings, so normally I nap.

As terrible as my job is, I'm not very bad at the role. I've always been better at giving advice than living it.

When a caller starts to trail off and I can tell they are about to terminate the call, I just ask about their day. No one listens to these people, and they'll gladly pay any number of cents per minute to be heard for a while.

If this doesn't work, I just ask what they're wearing. You can imagine where that goes.

Travis doesn't go to the river anymore. He doesn't respond to my text messages or stop by my house either. I didn't see him after I hugged him for too long, he made it clear what he learned — no need to report back. While I manage to convince myself that this doesn't affect me, it does in a dramatic way.

Olive

It serves as another painful reminder that every time I let someone get to know me too well, allowing them to take too close of a look past the surface, they go running away. Every time.

Hold an egg in your hand, extremely gently at first.

Begin to apply pressure, slowly.

Squeeze it progressively tighter, increasing the pace at which you do so.

When the shell finally cracks, and you have nothing more than a mess and a hand that needs to be washed thoroughly, you'll know exactly how it feels to know me too well.

At the river, I see flashes of Travis in the corner of my eyes. Darting quickly out of the frame, disappearing with ghostlike grace. He haunts me, but he probably can't even remember my name.

There are ghosts everywhere now.

Just like every home I've ever had. They're hiding in the walls, behind the pots and pans, behind every closed door in this city.

The need to run is as present as ever, the ability to do so is no longer even fathomable.

Fall is in the distance, but summer remains heavy in the air.

While on the hotline, I smoke pot so that I'm slower to

respond. More drawn out. Thoughts take a few seconds to assemble, and it fits the vibe that people expect when calling in for long distance mystic advice.

I drag on the introductions, trying to catch hints of where the reading should steer. The hotline has its own digital Tarot deck that they prefer you use, but I flip over some Tarot cards that I picked up second hand. I never bother to attempt to learn their imagery or connect with their (alleged, though never apparent) energy. I just wing it.

These cards, caller, represent your current situation:

Nine of wands. *You're uncertain, you feel like you're tired from all of the hard work you've done, but new challenges are springing up left and right. Even harder challenges, because the last battle was one that you were equipped to deal with. This is where you are now, is this speaking to you?*

It's always speaking to them, and I'm always speaking to myself.

Judgement. *This is card 20, part of the Major Arcana. This is a very powerful card, and you have some very powerful things crossing you. Everything begins now, as well as ends. It has all led up to this, and you're not sure how the fuck to cope with it. This is new. You can't fly under the radar anymore. A brand new battlefield…*

You don't call into such a hotline when everything is going as planned, after all.

Let's move in to cards that represent the current

obstacles.

The King of Cups, *no surprise here. You thought everything was going as planned, and you were finally pulling off the role you've been trying to play. Perfecting it even. This confidence is the footing that you've lost.*

I'm too caught up now to check in for a progress report with the customer, and sometimes, if you really get going, they'll get caught up too and stop searching for connection in each detail, but instead grasping for the big picture with you. Get them there and they'll stay on the line all night.

Page of Wands, *that's you alright, but it's reversed. You thought you had your new skill mastered, but you're actually not very good. No offence... you have the potential to be good.... there's a lot of talent in these cards, I can see that. You just aren't taking **it** by the horns... whatever **it** is. You have all of the tools to take it where it needs to be, but you're meandering. Or at least that's how you're feeling,*

Am I talking in circles? I'll ask this out loud,

Am I talking in circles? *Is this giving you anything at all?*

"Oh!" a voice will say on the other end. "You're on fire! You're exactly right! Oh! This is creepy."

I take this opportunity to tell the caller I require a few minutes to collect the energy that I've gathered from the cards, and that this reading is very strong. It can be exhausting, I'll say.

I'll brush my hair. I'll grab a half-smoked joint from the ashtray. The window is already open, so I decide I'll step onto the roof, grabbing my unturned cards and cigarettes on my way out.

I'm lighting a candle for you right now, one that will send you strength and clarity, I'll say as I flick on the lighter and take the a long puff from the partial joint.

Eventually I lose the call. I hear car doors very loudly and I say, *The cards are telling me there will be an unexpected knock on your door, and if we get disconnected don't forget my name is*— and like clockwork the knock comes and the caller hangs up frantically. I decide to continue reading the cards anyhow, because I think they were coming through more to me than the caller.

Two of Wands, *reversed. A fear of the unknown. A lack of solid plans.* Check.

Ten of Cups, *reversed. A questioned moral compass. A broken home or heart.* Check.

Nine of Swords. *A heavy head, wracked with anxiety and uncertainties. A great depression, an unlifting fog.* Check, check, check.

Nine of Cups, *reversed. This card represents being burdened by greed and material objects. A burning desire to expel these items from your life.*

Outside the sun is heavy in the air, *and this why people*

move to Sweden, I'll tell myself as I roast on the roof — the river full of furniture and remnants of abandoned small appliances just barely in view.

These cards, I remind myself, *these are the final outcome.*

Knight of Cups.

I didn't see that one coming.

The Knight of Cups is smooth and sincere in his actions. He has charm and a vivid imagination. He is, quite literally, a knight in shining armor. **This is sure to be a cat.**

The Wheel of Fortune. *The wheel is always moving, going up and down like an out of control Ferris wheel. Everything is up in the air, but everything will always reach the surface. Good things are at the end depending on how you hold up. Remember this,* I remind myself again, *remember this.*

Now employed, I grow accustom to the company of over the counter speed: Available on Amazon. Two of these little yellow decongestants in the morning is the only way the hot days can seem tolerable. And a few puffs off a joint is the only way I can handle the sensation, so I spend my days in my home office in a stimulated sedation.

I've set up a desk at the end of the hallway, right in front of the window. If I put the desk here, I can see when the mail arrives — and if I watch the mail arrive I can normally tell if there are more magazines.

I pray for days without magazines.

Occasionally I'll get some gifts for reaching high quotas at work.

A pendulum.

Some crystals.

Enough incense to kill a colony of cockroaches.

The pendulum hangs here in the window, throwing bright rays of color into my eyes as I stare at the giant, dim computer monitor that I salvaged among other relics of the 1990's in Shirley's room.

Upon setting up this computer for work, I finally found myself staring into the Internet for the first time in months. I felt that maybe I should Google something, but I couldn't think of anything worth Googling.

A yellow ray hits my eyes at 2:30 PM and it's time for one more pill. Maybe two, it's unacceptable to go to bed before dark anyhow.

Another puff of weed and another caller. This afternoon I'm casting runes.

The Birch Goddess. *The most obvious truth is hidden deep within, and only you will ever know it.*

A baby? A spiritual rebirth? A reawakening? A change of seasons within your life. Is this ringing any bells, caller?

ᚼ

The hail rune. *Don't try to fix what we should break before it breaks us.*

One more yellow pill. I'll put a little extra gin in my dinner to get to sleep tonight.

Don't put too much weight in being broken, dear. We're all broken in one way or another. Focus on your outstanding ability to mend. A tree has the same ability, but trees take centuries to repair.

The sun goes down, the olives come out. As promised, I pour a little extra gin in tonight so that I'll eventually be able to sleep. I'll sit and watch the river, from the roof tonight, but I'm too drained from my morning in the hot hallway to walk anywhere tonight.

The big thing right now with phone psychics is palm readings. I know this sounds absurd, because it truly is. In theory, people use their amazing camera phones to take a photo of their hand and email it in. These cameras are so nice and the photos are so well composed that you can hardly tell the hand isn't in the room.

What happens is, you get an inbox full of static-filled, dimly-lit photos of disembodied limbs that may or may not be hands at the beginning of each shift, and you're expected to call them when you're not on other readings.

A lot of drunks sign up for this while watching infomercials in the night, and when you call them the next morning at work they are rarely pleasant.

Other people, people without lives who obviously haven't moved from in front of the television since they sent the photo in, are typically more responsive.

"Oh, yes, I'm very interested to hear what you have to say on this. I've always been told I have very powerful hands. Dominant, even. Tell me what you see."

To be honest, I don't see anything. I don't even have the photo pulled up, and if I did it would be too distracting. It would just remind me that I have no idea what I'm talking about.

Thomas, is it? Thomas, take a look at your hand with me now. Make sure it's the palm that's in the photo that we're looking at here.

"Sure, sure."

You see that longest line? Notice how it's not only the longest but also the deepest, by quite some margin?

"Mmmhmm,"

That's your life line, Thomas. I can tell that you've had a long life that's seen a lot of hard work. Honest work, work that really pays off.

"Well, I can't disagree with that,"

Of course you can't, Thomas.

All of those other lines represent major events that have taken place along the way. You know, big things — advancements...weddings...kids...death, surely some of these must sound familiar?

"Oh yeah, sure thing."

That's all there is Thomas.

These callbacks cost $35, flat rate. No need to retain the customer any longer than absolutely necessary.

"So there's nothing about my future?"

Your palms only tell your story so far Thomas, the future is held in other oracles. I could read your cards or runes, but I do have to tell you that it would be an additional fee.

Thomas's silence indicates uncertainty, so I throw out a last ditch attempt.

A full reading is pretty intensive, but I could read one card for an additional 8 dollars.

He takes the bait. And what do you know, it's my favorite card:

The Fool. *A man has his possessions thrown over his shoulder, and marches bravely forward — paying no* *mind to where he is going. The Fool is walking off a cliff, but if he did not find himself here he would instead find himself in a place worth leaving. The Fool encourages you to follow your heart, and let your brain do other, more important, tasks. Your brain tells your heart to beat after all, so it isn't totally missing from the equation. The Fool is card 0, caller, but some of the oldest decks listed it as card XXII. 2+2 is 4, and since each numeral is repeated twice you should multiply that 4 by 2, which gives you 8. Keep 8 close to you, hold it tight like it's a secret that you don't want to forget. It will serve you well.*

Caller? I'm looking really far into this crystal ball, but I'm still not seeing you. I'm going to have to ask you to really focus on the visualization that we created. Okay? Make sure you're focusing on all of the details we discussed. To be clear, there is no crystal ball.

"I'm sick of visualizations."

I'm sick of visualizations too, though mine probably differ greatly.

What are you wearing, caller?

This question can go one of two ways. If it goes the right way, I can keep them on the line at least 8-12 more minutes. If it doesn't, they either end the call immediately or I convince them that poly-cotton blends could be blocking my psychic energy.

Temperance, reversed. *You're tired of taking vacations from your problems with panic-alleviating substances, but you're terrified to get back on with your life.*

The Moon, *reversed. Everything….I'm sorry, has everything been going to shit lately?*

"Everything has been fine...actually...I think I should go."

Call terminated...but why not:

Nine of Wands, *reversed. Paranoia. Hearing voices. Rough times ahead.*

The spirits are screaming loud and clear tonight.

I can't sleep. Perhaps it's the residuals of yellow pills or the lack of pot, but when I close my eyes its cluttered by knights and cups. Pentacles and towers. My bed is no longer a suitable environment for sleeping. I'll lay in the hall for a few hours, and then in the kitchen, before finally admitting the defeat and returning to the bed, falling asleep immediately.

The phone is already ringing nonstop when I open my eyes.

Change your career. Start over completely, it's time for a total change in your life if you ever want to move forward.

Today, I'm just giving myself advice out loud. No oracles

required.

You need to move. Pack everything you need into one box and put it on a train, then take a bus to the same city as the train and never look back.

I say this despite the fact that I'm in the middle of knowing that this plan doesn't end well. But the only thing I ever seem to learn from my mistakes is how to repeat them.

Identify five things that you love, remove everything from your life that does not relate directly to these five things. They could be foods, activities, even sleeping. Especially sleeping. Devote your life to only these four things plus sleeping for as long as you can and take note of what you learn.

Schedule your day, no matter how ridiculous the tasks you schedule are. Do your best to stick to this schedule. If you allow yourself 15 minutes to drink tea — take the entire 15 minutes and drink as much tea as you can. Remain firm in this commitment to commitment.

"But I don't see how this relates to the Queen of Cups."

From the Queen's lips to your ears.

The caller terminates.

Giant cats circle my house. They've replaced the rabbits of the spring. These are no house cats, and are easily three times the height of a house cat — but slender and athletic in build. Their eyes are piercing and intimidating, and they lock with my own while I sit at my desk.

Olive

They're after something, but I'm the only thing here. Just me and an empty pint of cheap gin, a half eaten jar of olives, and a magazine archive worthy of being in a museum.

At my desk, I attempt to write.

But to write feels too self-indulgent, too intimate of a use of my time for comfort. Something mindless is preferable, because who can't use some extra time to escape from their troubles.

To write would be to face them head on.

To walk to the river would require far too much energy, as each block seems to feel a mile longer than the last. By the time I reach the rushing water, even it doesn't have enough energy for the both of us.

And there are ghosts at the river. But there's ghosts in the walls and in the cupboards, and they're also found in the homes of every person who calls a psychic hotline. Probably many of the homes of people who don't call as well.

We're all just looking for ways to keep our ghosts at bay, keep the past buried — maybe stuffed in the back of some dusty attic or moist basement.

They're covered in cobwebs and trash bags, ripping at the corners with holes from jagged picture frames and journals.

Or maybe they're on the bookshelf, hidden behind the nonthreatening titles that you rave about to your friends, too afraid to loan one out, in fear that someone will see what's hidden behind.

These ghosts are on smells left on items at the bottom of your closet, items you'll always manage to avoid when doing the laundry. Items that you'll stand over and wonder, how many more times can I stand over this before I can be done. There is no magic number, but 8 seems as good as any.

Ghosts aren't just in the corner of your eye, they're in the back of your mind and now, thanks to the modern age, reflected in screens that are placed in front of your face.

You wait for them to speak, always scaring you when they do but at the end always leaving you more terrified that you'll never hear them again.

They can be hard to part with, and I think that's why we all keep so many merely hastily hidden. Among other relics, waiting to jump out and scare you — but you always know it's there.

I'm working on a new piece of advice for my callers, and it sounds something like this:

***Collect all of the items that contain ghosts** from your house. Be painstaking in doing this, and if you feel that a ghost could have transferred energy onto something near it or even vaguely related to it, bring all associated* *items. Once you've done this, take all of the ghosts to a river.*

A lake or pond or ocean will not do. Washing ashore soggy and disfigured or sinking directly to the bottom is not a fate suitable for these items. Take your ghosts and throw them into the river, preferably into an area where they will smash into a rock but then continue to float away in the rapids.

Go home. Be free. **This is how you kill a ghost.**

Rose flavored coffee and tealeaf-infused baths. Jasmine scented incense and fake lavender from my neighbor's dryer sheets.

My life feels too fragrant, too burdened by these floral aromas. Today feels like a lost cause, and it's raining but only in a pathetic attempt. 1:00 PM feels as good of a time as any to go back to bed.

A caller named Travis comes through. The ghosts have found their way into my phone line.

What's your birthday, Travis?

"November 20th."

Conceived in late winter, born in late fall. Always destined to be late to meetings and fall out cold at the end of the night, just as the sun begins to rise.

Two of Swords. *Someone cares very deeply for you.*

"I don't know that this is true."

Of course you don't know, you're a blind man searching the world aimlessly. Stumbling around, looking so hard for what is right under your nose. You don't see your problems or their solutions. Everything has presented itself to you and you're too afraid to face it head on.

Travis hangs up.

Next caller. Donna. Divorcee. Heavy smoker, from the sounds of it.

These crystals say your health is at risk. Your throat chakra is screaming for help. Stop smoking, stop drinking, stop crying all of the time. Introduce positivity into your life and it will surely multiply.

I have long given up on attempting to tell callers what they want to hear. This may keep them on the line a little longer, but to be inauthentic is too much of a burden to bare.

All emotions encourage art if experienced in the right way. Bitterness may be the most prolific and piercing, and anger may scream inspiration at the loudest level, but they're no different, really.

Try and experience every emotion to the same level

at which you experience these negative ones. How do you achieve this? Throw away your medication, drop the calming rituals, abandon anything that alters you if it does so in a stifling way.

Give up on attempting to have a sleep schedule that seems remotely human. Eat only when you have to, and only eat things that can be consumed in one brave, satisfying bite. These actions will bring power into your veins, and fire (*perhaps even misfire*) the circuits that have long been sleeping behind your eyes.

When being awake is necessary, achieve this state by overdosing on strong black coffee and pale yellow pills.

Sleep will only be a challenge when it is required, otherwise you can barely keep your eyes open — despite all of the substances you consume in an effort to do so.

Only answer the phone on the third ring. If you miss the third ring, you've already missed the call. It'll be someone else's problem to deal with.

"I'm Brenda....I don't know where to go...I just want to be well."

Wouldn't we all.

Brenda, I can't help you. If you can't tell me what time you were born I have no way of knowing where you're supposed to be. This is very important information, it's on your birth certificate. Don't worry, I'll stay on the line while you locate it.

These things take quite a while to find.

The time at which we were born and the stars that were shining on that night control every experience that you will have in the rest of your life. This is what I've read, anyhow. It seems like as good of a thing to believe in as anything else.

While I wait, I'll research what star I was born under, and this is what I'll find:

Theemin

(Upsilon 1 and 2 Eridanus)

5 degrees from midheaven. This red giant star, in the constellation of the River, is said to give the ability to succeed in scientific pursuits.

Even the constellations in my sky are going to end up downstream. Fate is written in the stars. Science eludes me, even though the stars are where I've decided to seek my advice.

My father calls unexpectedly, on my own abandoned cell phone — not the psychic hotline. I'm not even sure how he got my number, and from the sound of him he wasn't sure either. At first I thought maybe I was mistaken and he had called the hotline, and upon realizing it was him I skipped the introduction.

"Where are you?"

Wisconsin. The dairy state. I've taken a liking to cows and silos. I ride a cow around town, it's much cheaper than a car.

"I bet the maintenance is cheaper too, what are you doing with your life?"

The same thing I'm doing right now. I talk to lonely people on the phone in the middle of the night and get paid by the minute. Except for right now I'm not being paid.

The questions stop here. I do not bother with clarification, as such would require clarity.

"Are there pine cones in Wisconsin? When the weather starts to change I want to start selling pine cones. I can get $10 a pop for big ones, selling them to the tourists. I could cut you in if you could find pine cones there. They'd be dirt cheap to mail."

A noble attempt to save me, but I let him know that I'm not familiar with the variety of trees in my region.

"Just open your eyes next time you step outside. There's so much to see, you can't miss it."

My father lives in the woods in some state that starts with an M. Missouri? Montana, maybe? Not Minnesota. Maryland? Maine? Massachusetts? Some state with pine trees and tourists, apparently. There are too many states that begin with the letter M, but maybe if we rename half of them it will make the others a little more memorable.

For the rest of the night, I'll talk to callers from other uninteresting states. Brenda calls me directly, stating that she's found her birth time and demands answers.

Move to a state that begins with the letter 'N', Brenda. There are more than half a dozen to choose from, half a dozen exactly if you don't count North Carolina, because that would be a mistake for you. But I do encourage you to think north.

As fall finally begins to arrive, I take to wearing only pale orange clothes and taking pills of the same color. I'll soak my olives in grapefruit juice, and maybe to celebrate the end of summer I'll buy a bottle of champagne. If I can ride in on a wave of disconnectivity and confusion, maybe I can pull it all together by the time the season has changed.

Mercury is in retrograde, and before I became a phone psychic these words never meant anything to me. Now, in placing my fate on the stars, I feel a sense of security, no matter how false it may or may not be.

The Wheel of Fortune continues to turn, and with each day that passes it seems more likely that it will turn in my favor.

There is an endless number of Tarot cards, countless clouds of cigarette smoke, and too many shards of shingles in my legs.

I'm pretty sure everything is going to be okay.

Life operates like some out of control Ferris wheel.

Olive

Circling rapidly and reversing suddenly and frequently.

Within one day, I can conquer the world and walk off the edge. Within one evening, if the stars are right.

The moon, which had been pushing down on me with as much force as it takes to move the tides, is suddenly both so close and so weightless. The Moon is no longer reversed. Hundreds of pounds of pressure have been lifted, and slowly the bags under my eyes and sweat on my brow will be as well.

My malingering anxiety and sadness has stepped outside of the view of the camera.

Rebirth is in the air.

At long last, with much resistance and lingering, summer is coming to an end, and autumn is falling into place.

I accidentally leave myself voicemails. I listen back to them later, to hear myself rambling and shuffling about.

Shirley's friends, who are in a Minnesota based punk band, crash at the house on Thursday on the way home from tour.

I have the air conditioner off and every window in the house open. Fall is alive in the breeze and I can feel the river in the air.

In an attempt to be a good host, I collect a few extra blankets and pillows from Shirley's room.

Peter, the drummer, helps me with this and spots the impressive magazine collection immediately.

"Holy shit, National Geographic?! I read these nonstop on the road."

He digs into the pocket of his ripped, unwashed jeans.

"I don't have any cash but I've got like an eighth of weed here, can I buy some of these magazines?"

I don't feel right about selling Shirley's things, but I insist he take a few copies of National Geographic. *Report back and tell me what you've learned*, I tell him as we smoke a joint while looking through the covers for interesting headlines.

"Shirley says you moved here to write a book, something about olives? Is it a cookbook?"

I suppose you could say that. It's turning out to be a cookbook for the mentally ill. I'm almost done with the research.

The next morning the house is cluttered with empty beer bottles and abandoned pillows, and the bag of pot is sitting on top of a note on the kitchen counter.

Thanks for the words, it says.

Selling but never exchanging words.

Olive

Selling but never listening to my own advice.

Selling direction, misinterpretations of Tarot cards and crystals. I seem to be in high demand, but I constantly feel like a telemarketer. Being hung up on every few minutes for trying to sell some service that is no good for anyone now.

But telemarketers don't have access to the same information as I do, and I could be halfway around the globe before my callers knew their credit card had been compromised.

And it's tempting, many phone psychics go to jail for this each year.

It's tempting, but how can you balance the karmic scales when you're weighed down by stolen identities and unpaid debts?

This call is a safe place. It may be recorded for quality assurance and training purposes, but it is a safe place nonetheless. The energy and information that we share here is unique to us, and we are protected by a glowing warm light that is too bright to be processed by human eyes. Caller, I encourage you to use this time to ask a question of the universe. You don't have to do so verbally, your thoughts are strong enough to keep the universe listening as long as you're in this space. So go ahead, ask something big, you don't get this opportunity often.

Everyone asks for the same things:

Fame

Fortune

A hot spouse

An even hotter sports car.

Everyone is so simple. So small-minded. Predictable.

I'll cut two inches off of my hair and wait for someone to notice.

Since I only communicate with others over the phone, no one will have noticed until long after this length has grown back and then some. Even then, I suspect they'll say: *You should get a haircut. It's amazing the difference these small steps make.*

Everyone wants you to be happy, just not bad enough to devote their time to the project or consider sacrificing some of their own happiness in return.

And why should they? Why should anyone who has worked hard enough to see the good spend their time squandering the sensation on someone who will never truly understand what to do with it.

Maybe, if I had it, I'd put it into a box and sit it on a shelf. I'd open it on days when I thought I could handle it. But never for more than a few moments. Never long enough to absorb any of it's light.

Fall took forever to arrive, but is gone in what feels like mere days.

The Wisconsin winter begins, and it is already too cold

Olive

for words, and the amount of snow that falls is truly mind-blowing. I fall asleep in fall, and when I wake up there is already more snow on the ground than I've seen in my entire my life.

I can get used to this, I tell myself. But it's not true. No human will ever grow accustomed to sub-zero temperatures, but I remind myself that at least it's not hot.

At least I'm not in North Carolina or New Orleans.

Winters in the Midwest are hard to survive without a car. Walking to a store is out of the question — even walking to the mailbox is too much these days. *This is the first time I've ever gone more than 3 days without checking the mail,* I remind myself. For the first few weeks of winter, Shirley leaves her boyfriend's every few days to bring me essentials, but once I reveal that olives, paper towels, and dish detergent can all be bought on Amazon, I stop seeing her as often. "It's just too cold to go outside. If the power failed tonight, we'd all die."

A month into winter and I'm plagued by frozen pipes and forgotten songs, the wordless disco melodies of which circle around my mind relentlessly.

On a Thursday, after some force that is apparent from the kitchen, Shirley slams her body into the front door, finally breaking through the thin seal of ice that has been keeping me stuck inside without my knowledge.

"This is too much for me. I think maybe I need to move east."

Where? Boston? New York?

"Fuck you. Maybe Karachi or Amman. Somewhere where I'm guaranteed to never see ice again unless it's in a glass, and even then only upon request."

Slow down your breathing. *Set an intention for our reading. Cultivate happiness with each breath. Do this not just during our call, but throughout your entire day. You have the power to manifest all of your desires — this power is just hidden. Lying dormant beneath the surface. Take a deep inhalation through your nose, and as you exhale through your mouth I'll draw your first card.*

The Devil. *Here is he, hidden within all of us. He manifests as addiction, frustration, a physical embodiment of feeling lost. The Devil's powers are strong, but no stronger than you are. The Devil is you, The Devil is me. He is the mailman, the passenger in your car. He is all of your friends and some of your enemies as well.*

Cold air continues to blow in from Lake Michigan, Shirley and the boyfriend that I still haven't met decide they can't handle another Wisconsin winter. They've decided to move somewhere tropical. Fiji or Costa Rica or Puerto Rico. Somewhere with palm trees and waterfalls and wildlife with warm blood. They'll be leaving in January, just as the terrible weather really begins to plateau with no signs of ending. They still haven't figured out the details, they're going to make it up as they go along.

Olive

This leaves me at an interesting crossroad.

With the money I've been making but barely spending, I have enough to disappear again and get by until I figure the next thing out or fail to do so.

I also assume I have enough money to stay where I am, take over Shirley's apartment, and finally throw all of the magazines into the river.

It feels insincere to choose just one of these options.

The air is getting colder and wetter with each day, and soon I'll have to worry that my sweat will freeze to my skin on walks home from the river, so I'll stop going at all.

I'll stop taking over the counter speed, and if I fall asleep during work. The good news is absolutely no one is watching.

This call may be monitored or recorded for quality assurance and training purposes, but no one else will ever hear these words.

On the third ring I answer, a caller asks for lottery numbers. He really needs the money. *Really, really* needs it.

Caller, are you in your kitchen?

He is.

In your pantry...are there olives? A jar or maybe a can?

I hear him opening the pantry door, rifling through canned goods. I hear him sitting aside corn and peas and pineapple until finally he says "Yes, yes there are olives here!"

The winning lottery numbers are on that can of olives. Maybe the UPC code...perhaps the expiration date. You should probably buy two tickets.

As luck would have it, I'm right. And a few weeks later the same caller ends up on my line. "I've been calling this line desperately trying to reach you all week. You were right. The numbers on the jar of olives...they won. I bought nine tickets, there are a lot of numbers on packaged food..."

And so, based on advice that was actually a joke, but allegedly now a premonition, this caller won a jackpot that is far more than most make in a lifetime.

"Since you gave me the numbers and the olives were from Italy, I want to buy you a trip to Italy. All expenses paid, the nicest hotel and the nicest restaurants while you're there."

I decline, but he insists that I take his number and give it some thought.

"It's the least I can do... if you need money and would prefer that I would understand...but I thought maybe a trip to Italy would be nice. The birthplace of Tarot — a free trip. Give it some thought."

Sure, I could use the money. Who couldn't? But it would be lost on me, the only things I can even think to spend my money on would only be destructive.

Olive

I make the mistake of mentioning this to Shirley the next day, and she stops the conversation and immediately takes control.

"You are out of your goddamn mind if you're even thinking of turning this down. Escape this tundra, I'll stay here and water the plants — go to Italy. I will never forgive you if you don't go to Italy. I'll take my magazines and I'll be out of your life forever."

And though the thought of a life without magazines does soothe me, I take Shirley's advice, and she decides to spend some time at home clearing out her things in my absence.

The caller pays for an expedited renewal of my passport. Within a couple of weeks, I'm on my first international flight. An experience I'd spent my entire life longing for, but somehow the idea of it barely excites me. *Not like this, this wasn't the plan.*

At the end of a very long day of travel, I arrive in Rome a few hours before sunrise. There is a sky full of clouds in the birthplace of stars.

I check into my hotel (*hotel seems too modest for this place, but what else do you call it?*) and quickly fall asleep on too-soft pillows and 2000 thread count sheets. I wake up after the sun has gone down, and in the lobby of the hotel I find a vending machine that sells cigarettes.

The old fashioned kind, with the lever underneath each familiar brand of smokes. I buy two packs of Marlboros and go back to my room.

Soon after arriving in my room, a knock comes on the door. I assume it's the hotel staff, informing me that they know I've been smoking in the bathroom.

I open the door, slightly, and see a waiter standing at the door with a thick silver tray. I open the door further.

On the tray, a bottle of champagne and a room service menu. A letter that will remain unopened. Compliments of the caller.

Upon confirming that the waiter speaks English, I tell him that I have severe food allergies and will only be eating olives, and that I would like a gin and tonic — but he didn't need to take the champagne away.

I alternate between smoking cigarettes while drinking champagne in the bathtub and smoking cigarettes while eating olives on the balcony. The view is lovely, and I convince myself to be thankful for this trip. While it may be nothing more than a change of scenery, it is, after all, not so bad.

Eventually, I pass out. I manage to wake up just after noon and, while trying to ignore mounting anxieties, I hurry out of the hotel.

Now in a coffee shop in Italy, a mere four blocks from my hotel, the room smells thick with cinnamon. *This isn't an authentic experience*, I tell myself, disappointed. The thought of Italy never excited me, but I convinced myself that I should travel whenever given the opportunity, and a free trip never caused any harm.

But I want a trip that's free of the tourist traps from the guidebooks and travel websites. Paid advertisements, cleverly disguised as rave reviews. Free from spiral staircases, abandoned baggage. From knowing glares that I'm no native.

I don't actually like coffee.

I don't like pasta.

I don't like cheese.

I don't like Italy, and I don't like being here.

I don't want to be here.

I'll go back to the hotel, convinced that the Italian experience is too much for me. *Too much too soon, it's better to just sleep.*

Shirley sends me an email:

Thinking of you while catching up on Reader's Digest headlines. A free trip to Italy. Olive capital of the world...you must be in pure bliss.

If only she were correct.

After several days spent not leaving the hotel, I use the last of my small stash of cash on a cab ride to the airport, where I'll spend the rest of my day. It is recommended that I arrive several hours before my flight, and this is my plan. But my flight is cancelled, and I'm seven hours away from the scheduled departure of my new flight.

I've always recognized airports as being extremely unique places. They are a contained physical manifestation of a transient space. Everyone you see is either coming home or going far away, and their bodies radiate an entirely different energy than usual. All of this energy, swarming around in one building, it can get a little overwhelming. Each step feels more weighted. Each breath seems more urgent.

It's a long day of waiting in the terminal with no money for food or liquor.

A kind man who is also en route back to Wisconsin shares his lunch with me, and I resist the nearly unfightable urge to pick out the many ingredients that I'm not a fan of. Such would be rude in the face of his selflessness.

Instead I take tiny, bird-sized bites. Reveling in disgust with each one.

He is the kind of man that I want to immediately give my most treasured possessions to. In my gut I feel that I can trust him, though he'd probably dismiss these knick knacks that I hold so dear as trash and dispose of them as soon as I were out of sight. My judgement has always been less than stellar, after all.

Another stranded passenger, this one drunk, eats several jars of baby food while making direct eye contact with me. There's no room for judgement here, because her eating habits are no further from normal than my own.

"So, did you get a chance to see all of the sights while you were in Italy?" My new friend asks.

Olive

I saw some sights. The view from my hotel bed, the view from my hotel bath. The view from the hotel balcony. There was so much to see, too much, really.

Caller, there is a message waiting for you. It is not actually for you, but it is waiting for you to accept your responsibility as the one who must relay it.

"Who am I supposed to deliver it to?"

Someone that you know well, one of the people closest to you in fact. I'm seeing the letter 'E' in their name... maybe not toward the beginning...

"Hmm...Yeah, okay, go ahead."

The ghosts are wearing them down. You need to tell them to fight the ghost with all of their strength. Avoiding the ghost will not do...scream at the ghost, hit the ghost, burry it in a field. Do whatever it is that you can do to scare the ghost away.

Love is all around, and it's making me sick. It's in the cards for every caller I speak to, and their total dependence on it doesn't sit well with me. Sure, it's fine if you can find it. But it only ever finds you if you're completely unprepared to receive it.

I'm sure all romance is this way, just a building series of resentments. I ask people to tell me how terrible their relationships are, just to assure myself that I'm better off without.

They're interesting, the things people tell you.

They all claim there is nothing wrong with the person they love. Then they list dozens of attributes of their significant other that just drive them absolutely insane, and then they end with how lucky they are to have them.

Shirley calls on a Sunday to tell me that we need to talk. I know this cannot be good news.

She shows up with two 40 oz beers and an unopened pack of cigarettes, "You might need these, I've got some news."

Based on the prior night's reading, I already know where this is heading:

Card 13: Death. *Literally a death of the old self, and the birth of a new one. New beginning, a fresh start. Time to start everything over again.*

"Eric and I have been having fine tuning our plans and we've decided to move to Hawaii. We're going to be work on a macadamia nut farm in exchange for room and board. I got the idea while watching Roseanne."

Wow is all I can muster. I know Shirley too well to suggest that moving to a completely different part of the world where the only person she knows is her on-the-rocks boyfriend may not be the best idea, and the opportunity to suggest as much has long passed.

I open one of the 40s and take a sip. *Well, that's exciting.*

Olive

You're going to need to update the address on a lot of magazine subscriptions. I smile. Shirley does the same.

"There won't be time for that. We've decided to leave on Thursday."

Beer stops halfway down my throat.

My mind is racing with questions of what to do. Where I'll go, where I'll live, how I'll ever afford to move. I knew this time would come, but I had no idea so many decisions would need to be reached so quickly.

And how would Shirley ever move her things by Thursday? Despite her best efforts to clear out her room during my trip to Italy, she had done little more than disrupt the order of the magazines that covered her bed.

Shirley interrupts my thoughts, "So, I don't know if I've mentioned the fact that my family owns this place and it has long been paid off."

No.

"Yeah...why else would I have moved here?"

I've never wondered this, it never occurred to me that Shirley hadn't picked this house on her own, and hadn't been paying rent all of this time. Suddenly her extreme lack of commitment to her home made so much more sense.

"My dad spent his first five years as a surgeon here, and this place was his first major purchase. He didn't even have a car...he walked to the hospital in the snow and would just stay at work until the warmest part of the day rolled around, can you imagine?"

I cannot.

So, do you think he'll sell the place?

Shirley shoots me a bewildered look, "Why, are you in the market?"

No. Just curious.

"He barely remembers that he has this place. Much less that I live here. So...unless you really want to move I wanted to let you know that you can stay here for as long as you want. Keep watering the plants, yeah? I mean, realistically, how long are me and Eric really going to make it? I'm guessing a tropical environment will only make things more tolerable for a few months at best. So, what do you say? You'd need to pay the bills, but it's never very much."

I'm not sure how to respond to this bomb that Shirley has dropped. To say I'm short on words would be an understatement.

I'm not sure what to say. That is so kind of you...I've never had anyone in my life who has been as supportive and amazing as you. I wish I could express the gratitude I feel for you.

In this moment I decide that once I've finally finished that book, I'll dedicate it to Shirley. And maybe I'll send a copy to Travis when I'm done, too.

Olive

Shirley lights a cigarette using the flame of a candle that sits on the table. *Every time you light a cigarette using a candle a sailor gets lost at sea*, I hear my grandmother say in the back of my mind, her voice as clear as if it were across the room.

"Don't mention it," Shirley says as she exhales. "Seriously, I don't want to hear it."

Shirley, I don't know how much faith you put in this stuff but...can I read your Tarot cards?

I light an amber incense and clear the wobbly coffee table. I hand her the deck, which has now become tattered and worn. She shuffles the cards, cuts the deck, and passes it to me. I deal the cards, and immediately they begin to loudly speak.

Here's what they have to say:

You're lost at sea Shirley, but all of the answers will unfold exactly as you need them. While I'm not sure that things will work out with Eric, the path you're on will lead you to the place you need to be. You're making improvements, and once you've finally become balanced you'll see blessing in an abundance.

I flip over a few more cards.

I'm seeing a lot of pentacles, so money will never be a problem. Either you'll always have more than enough or you'll never be bothered by the fact that you don't.

Three aces: Cups, Wands, Pentacles.

Every ace is a blessing.

Inspiration, manifestation, love and compassion.

All in abundance.

Elsewhere in the spread, **The Emperor** and **The Magician** sit starkly across from each other. The freethinker and the great power of those who conform. This seems to be a great struggle in Shirley's life, but the end result is clear.

Shirley's last card is **The Wheel of Fortune.** I haven't forgotten how good this is, but I'm hesitant to share that information with Shirley.

Instead, I look her directly in the eyes and smile.

Made in the USA
Charleston, SC
28 February 2016